Take It to the Max

by Dan Danko and Tom Mason
Based on the teleplay "Sacrifices" written by Greg Weisman

SCHOLASTIC INC.
New York   Toronto   London   Auckland   Sydney
Mexico City   New Delhi   Hong Kong   Buenos Aires

ISBN 0-439-22565-5

12 11 10 9 8 7 6 5 4 3   2 3 4 5 6/0

Printed in the U.S.A.
First Scholastic printing, December 2001

Chapter

1

Max Steel didn't expect a heat-seeking missile on a school day. But he was about to get one.

With an almost soundless *whoosh*, the N-Tek corporate jet cut through the clouds, several thousand feet in the air.

Inside, Jefferson Smith reclined in his jet's plush accommodations. The forty-seven-year-old head of N-Tek, and Max Steel's adopted father, ran a hand over his balding head. He couldn't relax. Running N-Tek, the extreme-sports company and secret antiterrorist organization, was tough enough at the best of times, but right now, he was more worried about his son than anything else.

Across from him sat Mari Keita, the secretary general of the United Nations. Since the UN had chartered N-Tek's espionage activities, Keita had technically become Jefferson's boss. At the moment, however, she had forgotten that she was his boss and watched him sympathetically.

"He's not a kid anymore, Jefferson," she reminded him.

"I know, Mari," Jefferson replied. "I know. But I still worry about him."

Jefferson looked through the open curtain to the cockpit. Max sat in the pilot's seat, handling the jet with skill surpassing any airline pilot. It had only been three months since the accident at N-Tek that had transformed nineteen-year-old Josh McGrath into the secret agent known as Max Steel.

"He'll always be a kid to me," Jefferson said, loud enough for Max to hear.

And Max did hear. He chuckled to himself and shook his head. That's when the missile showed up.

"Incoming!" Max yelled.

An alarm sounded in the cockpit. Max checked his radar and instantly veered the plane to the right. The missile rocketed past the jet, just missing it.

"A ground-to-air missile's locked on our heat trail!" he yelled toward the back of the plane. "And it's coming back for more."

The missile turned in front of the jet, ready to try its target a second time.

"Hey, bro," Max said through his comlink to 'Berto Martinez back at N-Tek's Team Steel control room. "Where are the armaments on my jet?"

Back at N-Tek, 'Berto looked sheepish. A child prodigy, 'Berto was one of the foremost experts in cybernetics, nano-technology, and biomedical research. Though his close-cropped hair and glasses made him seem like a bookworm, 'Berto was also a capable field agent, in spite of the fact that he was only eighteen years old. "They're not installed yet, *hermano*," he said, his voice echoing through the comlink and into Max's head.

"What?" Before Max could say more, Jefferson rushed in and jumped into the empty copilot's seat.

"What's our status?" he said.

As Jefferson fastened his seat belt, Max flicked a switch and left his seat. Jefferson grabbed the steering column in front of him, gripping it with both hands.

"You're flyin'. I'm fixin'."

"Josh! I mean Max! Wait a minute! What are you doing?"

Max just smiled. "Hero stuff." The Max-Probes in Max's body surged with power as he ran back toward the jet's exit door.

Chapter

2

"Yeeeeeee-hahhhhh!"

Max's thumb pressed a button on the console by the jet's open door. He grabbed the side of the door and stepped out, his feet attached to a sleek metallic skyboard that looked like a long snowboard. A small backpack was strapped to his back. Then he let go!

Max sliced through the air. He twisted his body and rotated his feet. The skyboard turned quickly left, then right, then left again, as he rode the air currents.

His arms glowed with Turbo Power from the Max-Probes. He reached into his utility belt and grabbed a safety flare. He snapped it in half, igniting it.

Inside the jet, Jefferson was glued to his radar screen as Ms. Keita entered the cockpit.

"The missile's getting closer," she warned. She pointed out the cockpit's window. Both she and Jefferson could see the approaching weapon.

Jefferson pushed up on the steering column, sending the jet into a dive. The missile turned down after it.

"I can't shake it!" Jefferson yelled, both hands on the steering column. "No matter what I do, it stays after us."

Riding the air currents like a surfer catching an ocean wave, Max sky-surfed behind the jet, carving the air at 30,000 feet. He was in total free fall, with only one chance for his plan to succeed.

Max twisted and turned his body in midair, waving the flare in front of him. The missile's heat sensors were

still tracking the jet. Max turned the skyboard and caught an updraft toward the missile. He passed right in front of it.

"Gotcha!" Max yelled to the missile.

"Max! What are you doing?" It was 'Berto coming through the comlink. Through the technological enhancements of Max and his Bio-Link connection, 'Berto could see whatever Max saw.

"Can't talk now, bro. I'm working on something for the highlight reel."

Max caught another wave of air and hurled his body into the missile. He slammed against the side of the missile and dug his fingers into the metal casing. He pulled his body toward the missile's nose.

"Follow this logic, bro," he said through his comlink to 'Berto. "What's a heat-seeking missile seek?"

"Max! Do you know what you're doing?" came 'Berto's reply.

"You're not answering my question." Max smiled.

With one hand holding onto the missile, Max waved the flare in front of the missile's nose.

The missile's heat sensors caught a whiff of the burning flare and that was all Max needed. He pushed himself off the missile with the flare in his hand. He was free-falling toward the water, 30,000 feet away.

"Come and get it!" Max taunted the missile.

Lured by the heat of the flare, the missile turned and followed Max. Jefferson straightened out the jet, resetting it for its original course toward Del Oro.

But the missile was still chasing Max. And getting closer. Closer. Closer. At the last second, Max tossed the flare down toward the ocean, like a pitcher throwing a hard strike.

But not quite hard enough. The missile dove onto the flare and exploded. The shock wave roared through the sky, stunning Max. Unconscious, he tumbled through the air toward the water. . . .

Chapter

3

"Max? Can you hear me?" It was 'Berto speaking through Max's comlink. "Jefferson wants you back at N-Tek for a debriefing on that missile."

"Got it. Just give me a minute," Max replied.

Following the explosion of the missile, Max's unconscious body landed in the waters of Del Oro Bay. An N-Tek search-and-rescue team was on the scene in less than two minutes.

But there was really no need for it. The Max-Probes that coursed through Max's body and fed on regular doses of Transphasik Energy made him stronger and tougher than any normal athlete. Even without "Going Turbo!" Max could take what that missile had to offer and more.

A couple of hours after the blast, Max was back to normal, in more ways than one. Using the Max-Probes, he had altered his body form and was no longer in his Max Steel identity. Now he was just Josh McGrath, nineteen-year-old extreme-sports athlete and college student at Del Oro University, one of the top twenty-five destination schools in North America.

In his jeans and T-shirt, his hair blond instead of

brown, Josh looked like any normal college student returning from summer vacation to start his sophomore year.

"It's just great having you back, Laura," Josh said to Laura Chen, the pretty Chinese-American girl in the passenger seat. With her shoulder-length dark hair and tremendously appealing features, she could easily be an actress. That certainly explained her drama major at Del Oro University.

"And it's great to be back, Josh," she replied. Laura had spent the summer between her freshman and sophomore year traveling on her own through China. "And having you help me move my stuff into the dorm."

Josh had parked his old T-Bird in front of Clemens Hall, his two-story campus dorm. As usual, he hadn't parked it very well: One wheel was up on the curb.

Josh exited the car carrying a tower of large storage boxes. Laura carried a couple of smaller ones, and a bag of still-warm french fries.

As he shut the car door with the back of his foot, Josh reached across Laura to snag a fry. But the boxes threw him off balance and Josh crashed to the ground, the boxes falling on top of him.

"Josh!" Laura exclaimed.

Josh pushed aside a couple of the boxes and peeked

out from underneath. "Nothing fragile, I hope," he said sheepishly.

"You're asking her now?" came a voice from behind the car. Laura and Josh turned to see Pete Costas smiling. Pete, his black hair blowing slightly in the breeze, was the same age as Josh. He was also Josh's best friend at Del Oro U.

"Pete!" Laura called out and raced to give him a friendly hug.

"Welcome back to Dormsville," Pete said. "How was China?"

"I missed this place . . . and I missed Josh."

They both turned to look at Josh. He stuffed a french fry in his mouth and picked up the boxes.

"Dude. How about a little help here?" he greeted Pete.

"Sure," Pete replied as he grabbed a couple of fries from Josh. "Those fries look awfully heavy."

Laura slipped in between the two of them, her arms around their waists. "Just like old times. The three musketeers together again! Did you guys get your old room back?"

"Ask him," Pete replied unhappily. "It was his idea."

"Okay, what's going on with you two?" Laura asked.

"I moved out of the dorm. Got my own place."

"You're kidding. . . ." Laura was stunned. Josh and

Pete had been roommates all through their freshman year.

"I'm renting a beach house," Josh said quickly. "You'll love it."

"Is there anything else you haven't told me, Josh?"

"*Hermano.* Now!" It was 'Berto on the comlink again.

Josh shrugged. He couldn't answer 'Berto with Laura and Pete standing so close. He wanted to tell Laura about his identity as Max, but he couldn't. It would put her at risk for kidnapping or worse from N-Tek's many enemies. And he wanted to tell Pete the real reason for the beach house: It had a light rail system that connected it to N-Tek's headquarters.

But he had to keep everything a secret, so all Josh could say was, "Um, nothing really. Same old."

Chapter

4

The sun was high over Del Oro Bay. Sitting just off the Pacific Coast Highway, it was one of the fastest-growing cities in the country. Spectacular beaches, an easy drive to the nearby Mount Corinth Ski Resort, and the shops and restaurants lining trendy Nathanson Avenue Promenade, Del Oro Beach had it all.

Nearly half of the town worked for N-Tek, whose corporate offices were just a ferry ride away on nearby McGrath Island. The island was named for Josh's birth father, one of the best antiterrorist agents N-Tek had ever had, but most people didn't know that part.

On the surface everything looked peaceful. The water sparkled like it was brand-new, barely rippling in the bright sunlight. But underneath, deep in the water, an electromagnetic car glided along a light monorail network.

Josh had gone back to his beach house, taken the secret elevator to the "basement," and grabbed a ride out to McGrath Island.

Inside the Plexi-car Josh sat, alone for the first time since the missile attack that morning. He remembered the first time he had discovered the secret of N-Tek. It wasn't the giant extreme-sports conglomerate that he had always thought. It was an antiterrorist organization, sanctioned by the United Nations. An organization that his biological father, Jim McGrath, had worked for prior to his death at the hands of N-Tek's founder, Mark Nathanson.

Josh had discovered N-Tek's secret by accident while trying to stop a burglary at the company's main office. He

had gone there for a late-night dinner with his adopted father, Jefferson Smith, but instead found himself confronting a mysterious metal-faced burglar. The ensuing fight left Josh unconscious and smothered by Max-Probes, microscopic machines that were absorbed into his body.

The machines would have killed him, but 'Berto came up with the idea of feeding them Transphasik Energy. That not only kept Josh alive, but it made him stronger, more powerful, almost invincible.

Like N-Tek had its secrets, Josh had his, too. During the day, he was Josh McGrath, a student at Del Oro University. But in his spare time, and when duty called, he used the Max-Probes in his body to alter his physical appearance and become . . . Max Steel, N-Tek's newest secret weapon.

The Plexi-car pulled into the underground station. The doors whooshed open and Max stepped out.

"You're late, Mr. Steel. Again." That cool English accent could only belong to one person — Rachel Leeds. Tall, athletic, and with short blond hair, she looked like a model but was actually one of N-Tek's best operatives — an experienced agent, and an expert in espionage and covert activities.

When Josh made the decision to join N-Tek's fight and take on the secret identity of Max Steel, Jefferson had assigned Rachel to keep an eye on him, to keep him out of trouble. Together, Rachel, Max, and 'Berto formed Team Steel, their own special unit of N-Tek.

Rachel grabbed Max by the arm and ushered him toward the terminus exit. "They're waiting for us."

"Cut me some slack, please," Max requested. "I pulled a major save this morning."

"You did your job," Rachel replied coolly.

"It wouldn't kill you to say 'Nice work, Max' would it?"

"Oh, quite possibly," Rachel smiled as she escorted Max down the hall toward the elevators that led to Jefferson's office.

As they entered, Jefferson was talking with Jean Mairot, the forty-year-old Frenchman who was the hands-on manager of N-Tek's operatives and agents, and 'Berto.

"Fortunately, the Cain Virus was isolated and contained quickly," Mairot said. He pointed to a picture of an African hospital that filled the room's giant monitor screen.

"The victims are quarantined in a Nairobi hospital," he continued. "We have them under 'round-the-clock surveillance. Agents Grange and Atebe are escorting a sample of the virus back here to the University Bio-Research Center. We expect them later today. Then our scientists can start to work on a cure."

Mairot stopped. He and Jefferson turned their attention to the doorway where Max and Rachel stood.

"Max, Rachel. Good. Jean and I were about to discuss this morning's . . . incident."

"No need to thank me," Max said sarcastically. "Rachel's been gushing."

"Any idea who launched the attack?" Rachel asked, ignoring Max.

"Dr. Yevshenko is backtracking the missile with Nez and Murtaugh," 'Berto spoke up. "We think we can pinpoint the launch site by studying satellite photos from the surrounding areas."

Mairot picked up a remote control and clicked it. On the monitor screen, the image of the Nairobi hospital faded away and was replaced by Mari Keita's picture.

"But our immediate concern is the intended target," Mairot indicated. "United Nations Secretary General Mari Keita."

"Are you sure?" Max said excitedly. "Couldn't the intended target also be Jefferson? This could be connected to the 'security breach' we had last June. If someone knows who Jefferson really is . . ."

"No one does," Jefferson interrupted. "To the world outside these walls, N-Tek is a sporting goods company. No one sends missiles after corporate executives who make skateboards and skis."

"Unless they hate skateboards and skis," Max quipped. Nobody but Max laughed. "Just a thought," he added. He knew his father wouldn't listen to him, anyway, so he just stopped talking.

"But the leader of the UN," Jefferson continued, "that's something else. There are any number of terrorist organizations, large and small, that could be responsible."

"That's where Team Steel comes in," Mairot said. "I have a list of safe houses in my office. We can put Ms. Keita in one of them and protect her until this is solved."

"Excellent," Jefferson said. "Now, could I . . . I'd like to speak to Max for a moment. Alone, please."

Rachel, 'Berto, and Mairot traded glances. *What's this about?* seemed to be the unspoken question. They turned and left, the door closing behind them.

As soon as the door slid shut, Jefferson threw his arms around his adopted son. "Josh," he exclaimed. "I was so worried when the missile exploded and you hit the water this morning."

"Aww, Dad, cut it out," Max blushed, embarrassed by this display of emotion.

Jefferson let go and backed up a step. Now it was down to business.

"I was *less* than thrilled with today's little stunt," he said.

"Got results. N-Tek 1, missile 0. Game over. We win."

"You're making a habit of taking insane chances," Jefferson said. "I can't have you putting yourself or Team Steel at such risk."

"Have you read my job description?" Max said, defensively. "Secret agent: lousy pay, insane chances . . . and no appreciation! Especially the no appreciation part!"

Angrily, Max stepped toward the door.

"Josh — Max — wait!" Jefferson called.

Max opened the door and stepped into the lobby. Jefferson stopped and lowered his head. Max slammed the door behind him.

Chapter

5

Mount Corinth was the tallest mountain in the area around Del Oro. In the winter, it was a world-class ski resort. And in the summer, it was perfect for mountain biking, hiking, and rock climbing. It might not be as tall, perhaps, as Kilimanjaro or McKinley, but climb it on a hot day, and it seemed just as steep.

It had taken most of the morning, but Dr. Elena Yevshenko and her team of Dr. Avi Ben-Rubin, Jake Nez, and Jack Murtaugh had reached the top of Corinth. Dr. Yevshenko stopped by a patch of charred ground surrounded by equally charred trees.

"Yevshenko to Mairot, come in," Yevshenko said into her radio headset. In her hand, she held a small scanner that beeped quietly and regularly.

"Mairot here, Doctor," came the reply. "Have you located the launch site?"

Of Russian descent, Dr. Yevshenko was N-Tek's resident science and technology expert. If anyone could find a trace of the missile launch, it would be her.

"Yes. The missile came from the top of Mount Corinth," she said as she looked down the slope. Huge tire tracks led down the mountain. "Tire tracks lead to the highway. It seems that Keita's faceless enemies own a mobile missile-launcher."

"Lovely," Mairot lamented over the radio. Now a missile could strike again and from anywhere.

While N-Tek's search team scanned the mountaintop for more clues, Max sped his convertible sports car, "Baby," down the Pacific Coast Highway. Baby was a "gift," courtesy of N-Tek's science lab. It was constantly being tinkered with and new gadgets were added to it all the time.

And just as Josh could transform himself into Max Steel, Baby could morph back into Josh's more traditional T-Bird convertible.

"Max, slow down," Rachel cautioned. "The secretary —"

"The secretary is enjoying the ride, Ms. Leeds," Ms. Keita interrupted. "You know, when the UN first chartered N-Tek, Mark Nathanson and Jefferson Smith took me on a tour of Del Oro, beginning on this very road."

Max steered the car, pushing the accelerator hard, like a NASCAR racer. Keita rode shotgun while Rachel was stuck in the not-so-spacious and not-so-comfortable backseat.

Rachel grinned playfully. "You've known Mr. Smith a long time, Ms. Keita. Have you ever met his son?"

Max frowned and shot a quick glance over his shoulder at Rachel. He was not happy. Rachel grinned. It was fun to see Max squirm a little.

"Josh? Of course. Mind you, I haven't seen him in a decade. He must be all grown up now."

"What was he like?" Rachel was enjoying this.

"Rachel . . ." Josh cautioned.

"A handful," Keita said thoughtfully.

"Really?" This was better than Rachel had hoped.

"But how could he not be," Keita reflected. "His mother . . . gone. Then his father."

Max nodded in silent agreement.

"If Jefferson hadn't adopted that boy . . ."

Without finishing her thought, Keita let her words drift off as Baby roared down the Pacific Coast Highway.

"I'm a grade-A idiot," Jefferson Smith said as he paced in front of his desk. Jefferson was in his office with Mairot, discussing his relationship with Josh . . . and Max. He picked up a photo of a young Josh in his baseball uniform.

"You'll get no argument from me," Mairot agreed.

"Jean, he turns me inside out."

"You're his father, Jefferson. Maybe not biologically, but certainly in every other way. I believe that comes with the territory."

Jefferson stood and headed for the door. "I need to make it right."

"Max is having dinner with Leeds and Ms. Keita at Café

Café on the Promenade," Mairot offered as Jefferson left the office. "You can still catch them."

Max pulled Baby up to the curb, across the street from Café Café. It was an outdoor café on the edge of the trendy Nathanson Promenade, a long stretch of street-front shops, boutiques, and clothing stores that was *the* place to be in Del Oro Bay. The street was named in honor of Mark Nathanson, the original founder of N-Tek.

Max opened the car door and started to get out.

"Danger, Will Robinson . . ." It was 'Berto on the com-link. "Scan the area, *hermano*."

Max looked around and when his eyes stopped just across the street, he didn't like what he saw. He jumped back into Baby and roared the engine to life.

"Max, what is it?" Rachel questioned.

"Can you believe it," Max fibbed. "No tablecloths. Intolerable for the secretary general of the UN."

The car zoomed away . . . just as Laura and Pete strolled up to Café Café. Max had made a clean getaway without being seen by his two friends.

"I can't believe that Josh just blew us off tonight," Laura said, disappointment hanging on every word.

"You know, he didn't even ask me to go in with him on the beach house," Pete said.

But Laura wasn't really listening — something, someone, had caught her eye at the front of the restaurant. Jefferson Smith stood by the outdoor tables, obviously looking for Josh.

"Mr. Smith. Hi," Laura said as she walked up to him.

"Ms. Chen. It's been too long," Jefferson said.

"Have you seen Josh tonight?" she asked.

Before he could answer, Jefferson's cell phone rang from his pocket. He pulled it out and answered.

"Excuse me," he said to Laura before turning his attention into his phone. "Smith."

There was no voice at the other end. But there was a high-pitched sonic blast that shot directly through Jefferson's ear. Laura and Pete couldn't hear it, but they saw Jefferson's face twist in agony. Crying out in severe pain, Jefferson dropped the phone and fell to the ground unconscious, knocking over a table as he went.

"Mr. Smith!" Laura exclaimed. She rushed to his side. Before she could reach him, she was pushed aside by someone.

"Out of my way," a man said. "I'm a physician." The doctor leaned over Jefferson's fallen body. "This man's had a heart attack!"

Pete rushed to Laura's side. She looked around for a phone.

"I'll call —" she said, but was interrupted.

"I just called 911," a bystander said as he cut in front of Pete and Laura. Approaching sirens wailed from down the street.

Within seconds, the ambulance squealed to a stop in front of Café Café. Two paramedics leaped out, carrying a stretcher. They pushed past Laura and Pete, forcing them to step back.

With military precision, they hustled Jefferson onto the stretcher, felt for a pulse on his wrist, then loaded him into the ambulance. It took just a few seconds, and the only evidence that they were ever there was Jefferson's wristwatch. It lay on the ground where he had fallen.

"Talk about rapid response . . ." Pete observed. "They couldn't have been here any faster unless they were psychic."

Laura bent down and picked up Jefferson's watch. The ambulance roared down the Promenade, its sirens blaring.

Inside the ambulance, one of the paramedics took Jefferson's pulse.

"He's alive, but out cold, sir."

"Excellent," the doctor driving the ambulance said. He reached around under his chin and . . . peeled off his own face! In its place was a face of cold metal, glowing red eyes, and a terrifying smile. It was Psycho . . . one of Dread's top operatives and a sworn enemy of N-Tek!

"Hey Max, I've been thinking. How'd they know that Keita was in that jet?"

That was 'Berto, again through the comlink. Max had finally found a decent place for dinner with Ms. Keita and Rachel, and after he had dropped them back at N-Tek he was heading for home.

After a day like today, he was looking forward to an evening walk on the beach and then a nice, long sleep.

"Dude, you're working overtime. It's not our shift. We're done for the day." Max morphed back into Josh. Baby had devolved back into Max's T-Bird. "Go off-line, bro. Go outside and go crazy."

"Crazy, *hermano*," 'Berto replied, not really believing. "Right. Bye!"

Minutes later, Josh pulled up in front of his rented beach house. Laura and Pete were pacing on the porch as Max pulled his car between Pete's Saturn and Laura's motorcycle.

"Hey, guys . . ." Josh started but didn't get to finish.

"Where have you been?" Pete demanded. "We've been sitting here for —"

Laura crossed in front of Pete and took Josh's hand. "Josh," she said quietly. "It's your dad."

Josh looked at her, confused. What was going on?

"He's had a heart attack," she said.

"What?" Josh exclaimed. "How? When?"

"At Café Café," Pete said. "Right in front of us. An ambulance took him to the hospital."

"Which one?" Josh demanded.

"We don't know," Laura said sadly. "We phoned around, but he isn't listed anywhere."

"It's like he's disappeared," Pete offered.

Laura held out Jefferson's watch. "The paramedics dropped this outside the café. Maybe they lost his wallet, too."

Josh studied the watch. He was thinking, the mental gears turning swiftly in his brain. He was no longer confused, he was angry. He didn't believe for one minute that Jefferson Smith had had a heart attack. But Josh had a plan. He just had to do something to get Laura and Pete out of his way so he could let Max Steel take over.

"We have to split up," Josh said, controlling his anger. "We can cover more ground that way." Josh started ushering his two friends toward their vehicles. "Check out every ER in Del Oro. If you find him, call me on my cell. I'll do the same."

Pete opened the door to his car and got inside. Laura swung her leg over her motorcycle and picked up her helmet.

"I don't think you should be alone right now, Josh," she suggested.

"Laura, please . . . it's the only way."

She nodded and put on her helmet. Josh hurriedly checked his pockets, patting them as he pretended to search for something.

"My cell phone! I must have left it in the house."

Josh headed up the porch steps toward the front door as he called back to Laura and Pete. "Don't wait for me! Go! I'll catch up!"

The two friends each gave a quick wave and then were off. Josh stood on the porch as they disappeared from sight. He quickly morphed back into Max Steel.

"'Berto? Are you there? Talk to me!"

Inside the Team Steel Ops room, 'Berto sat in front of his console. His main monitor was dark, shut down for the evening. A smaller monitor was on, however, and 'Berto was busy studying a 3-D chess move against the computer.

"It is your move, specimen," the computer said.

Before 'Berto could make his choice, the main monitor clicked on. It was Max's view of the porch, watching Laura and Pete speed away. "'Berto!"

"I'm here, *hermano*. You're lucky I have no life —"

"Jefferson's been snatched." Max had no time for any small talk. Not at a time like this.

Max rushed toward his car.

"What? How do you know that?" 'Berto said excitedly.

Max jumped into his car and roared the engine. He held Jefferson's wristwatch in one hand.

"Whoever took him deliberately ditched his wristwatch tracer," Max explained. "Contact Mairot."

Max slammed his foot on the accelerator. The car morphed into Baby as it raced off into the night, in the opposite direction from Pete and Laura.

Chapter

8

"This is a Code One Alert," Mairot said into his headset. "Diamond, Sharaabi — stay with Keita. All other available operatives . . . report in to me."

Mairot was at N-Tek's helipad, rushing toward the helicopter piloted by Rachel.

"Go!" he yelled as he stepped inside. Within seconds, the whirling blades lifted the chopper into the night sky.

Mairot settled into his chair and started receiving reports from his operatives.

"Mairot? This is Yevshenko. We've found something."

At the edge of Del Oro Bay, just below the Pacific Coast Highway, Dr. Yevshenko and Dr. Ben-Rubin watched as a large truck was towed from the water. The truck's shell was partially damaged, but through it Dr. Yevshenko could see the large missile-launcher in the back of the rig.

"Go ahead, Doctor," Mairot acknowledged.

"We've found the missile-launcher. They dumped it in the bay, about three miles from the airport."

"The airport . . ." Mairot said thoughtfully over the radio.

"Nez and Murtaugh are en route," Dr. Yevshenko declared. "They should be at the airport now."

"Good work, Doctor," Mairot congratulated. "Now I need you at UBRC. If you cover the Cain Virus's containment, I can put my agents on to Jefferson."

"Acknowledged."

Inside the helicopter, Rachel received a communication from one of the ground units.

"I just got word," she said to Mairot. "Nez found the ambulance. Abandoned. A vacant lot across from Terminal C."

Mairot spoke into his headset. "All agents. Rendezvous at Del Oro Airport. Let's shut it down and get Jefferson back."

Chapter

9

"It's clean."

Mairot and Rachel watched as operatives Nez, Murtaugh, Maya Atebe, and Martin Grange picked through the abandoned ambulance, searching for any clues to Jefferson's whereabouts.

"Four private planes have departed to various international locations since the abduction," Rachel said. "Jefferson could be on any one of them."

"I've deployed Janawicz and Skarsgaard to Afghanistan," Mairot said as he turned to his ambulance crew. "The rest of you will be playing catch-up."

Mairot looked at the sheet that listed the four flights. "Grange, Atebe — you're going to Belfast. Nez, Murtaugh — Belgrade."

The agents turned and were gone. They had their assignments.

"Leeds, you and . . ." Mairot paused and looked around. "Rachel, where is Max?"

"If it was my father . . ." Rachel offered, without completing her sentence.

Mairot nodded. "All right, it's you and me. Let's move."

*   *   *

"Max, this is insane," 'Berto exclaimed. "Where are you going?"

"Off-roading," was Max's reply.

He was powering Baby up Mount Corinth. He had a hunch and it was taking him right to the missile-launch site that Dr. Yevshenko had discovered.

"Smith is not on Mount Corinth," 'Berto said. "He has to be on one of those four planes."

"Doubt it, bro," Max disagreed. "Check the evidence. Wristwatch, rocket-launcher, ambulance, airport. It's too easy. This trail's like bread crumbs for Hansel and Gretel."

"Okay, so what are we doing way up here?"

"This is where it all began," Max explained. "Where they tried to nail Dad with that missile. I think the fake heart attack and the ambulance grab was just Plan B."

Max pulled Baby into a clearing and jumped out. He followed the mobile missile-launcher's tracks in the dirt so that 'Berto could see what he was seeing.

"See?" Max pointed out. "There's only one set of tracks — and they lead *down* the mountain."

"Then how'd they get the missile-launcher there? Helicopter drop?"

"I don't know yet. But somehow . . ."

Max didn't get a chance to finish his thought. Underneath his feet, the ground rumbled. A second later, it started opening up beneath him. A trapdoor!

"Max! What's going on!?"

"The ground — it's swallowing me up!"

And swallow him it did. Max lost his footing and fell through the trapdoor, hurtling into the darkness.

"Ouch!"

Max hit the ground, hard. The trapdoor clanged above him, closed.

Standing up, he realized he was inside Mount Corinth now, only it didn't look like the inside of a mountain. There was no dirt, no rocks, no dripping water. Just shining steel and chrome. It looked like a high-tech industrial plant. Obviously one of Dread's secret bases.

A fist punched Max in the jaw, knocking him backward. He recovered quickly. Four of Dread's guards moved toward him. Max grabbed one by the arm and effortlessly flung him into another one. They fell to the ground, unconscious.

Max felt his arms pinned to his sides. The third guard had snuck around behind him. He bent down and flipped the guard over his head.

"Three down, one to go," Max said, pointing at the final guard. "Care to try your luck?"

The guard rushed toward Max. Max leaped into the air, spinning, his foot connecting with the guard's chin.

Max landed on the ground like a cat. He had hardly

worked up a sweat. "Quality beats quantity," he chuckled to himself.

Then Max heard the sound of footsteps on the metal floor. *Lots* of footsteps. He looked up and saw dozens of Dread's guards rushing toward him.

Max took a deep breath and launched himself into the mass of rushing guards. Within seconds he was buried underneath them. The guards' arms were punching, their legs kicking. But not for long. Max's fist emerged from the pile. One of the guards flew off. Then another. Then a third.

Max held an unconscious guard by the arms, spinning him rapidly in a circle. The guard's feet were batting away the other guards as quickly as they stepped into the circle.

Almost as soon as it started, it was over. Max flung his "bat" across the floor. He smiled . . . but only for a second.

"You!" Max was shocked, almost afraid, by what he saw approaching him. It was the second time that Max had seen him — the first time was as Josh McGrath, when this "walking nightmare" had thrown him against the vat of Max-Probes.

Now that grinning thief stood in front of him. Max was horrified to see him again.

Psycho marched right to Max, his metal face grinning broadly. He carried a fully charged shock-stick. "Have we met before?"

A second meeting with the man who had nearly killed him hadn't been covered in Max's last three months of training. Too stunned to move, Max stood frozen. Psycho took advantage and pressed the shock-stick against Max's chest. Max screamed in pain as he dropped to the ground like a crash-test dummy.

"You look so shocked to see me!" Psycho laughed, then kicked Max's limp body once, just for fun.

Chapter
11

Where am I, and why does my head hurt so much?

That was Max's first thought as he regained consciousness. He rolled over on his back. Big mistake. He groaned in pain.

Max lay on the floor in a small cell. He opened his eyes, looked around . . . and smiled. A familiar face was looking back at him from the next cell.

"Da — uh, Mr. Smith," Max corrected as he saw Jefferson Smith in a separate cell. "You're alive!"

"And so are you, Mr. Steel," Jefferson replied, all business. "Now where's your backup?"

"Looking for you in all the wrong places," Max said. "But don't sweat it. 'Berto's always right with me, right bro? Uh . . . bro?"

There was no response from Max's comlink. Jefferson looked frustrated, afraid for his son now that they were both trapped underground.

"The cell must be com-secured," Jefferson suggested. "Maybe the whole base." Jefferson paused. When he resumed talking, there was more than a little anger in his voice. "Why didn't you follow N-Tek procedures? Why didn't you obey your training? How could you come here alone?"

Max didn't take the criticism well. "Was I supposed to sit this game out?" he asked.

Max glared at Jefferson through the bars of the cell. Jefferson quickly realized there was only one thing left to do and say. "What do you say we escape now, argue later?"

Max nodded, revealing the slightest hint of a smile. "Now that's something I know how to do." He gripped the cell door with both hands.

An alarm beeped in the control room of the underground base. The words "cell breach" flashed on the mon-

itor screen. One of the guards pressed a button on the console and spoke into a microphone.

"Security breach in the brig."

Four guards raced down the hallway toward the cell. Their shock-sticks were charged and at the ready. No prisoners were going to get past them.

When they arrived at the cell, they stopped, shocked. Max and Jefferson were leaning slightly against their cell doors. Only now, Max was in Jefferson's cell and vice versa.

"There a problem, gentlemen?" Max teased the guards.

The leader of the guards looked around. There was certainly no problem that she could see. Max and Jefferson were still locked in their cells. The guard spoke into her helmet-microphone.

"False alarm."

She and the other guards turned to go. Then she stopped and turned back toward the cells. The other guards stopped, too.

"Wait a minute," she said thoughtfully. "Wasn't the old guy over there?"

"We got bored. So we switched," Max said. As he spoke, he and Jefferson shoved the bars of their cells. They weren't leaning on their cell doors, they were holding them up. The unhinged doors slammed out and into the guards, knocking them to the ground, unconscious.

"Old guy?" Jefferson said incredulously.

"They just have to learn respect for their elders," Max joked.

Max and Jefferson ran out of their cells. Jefferson stopped to remove a helmet from an unconscious guard. He put the helmet on his own head and spoke into the microphone.

"We're moving the prisoners," he spoke into the inset microphone. "Activate the knockout gas!"

"Gas?" Max whispered to Jefferson.

Jefferson pointed to the ceiling. Several nozzles hissed and spewed out a visible gas that started to fill the cell.

"I saw the nozzles while I was waiting for you to wake up. So I played a hunch."

"Took an 'insane chance,'" Max said with more than a hint of sarcasm.

Jefferson shot a glance at Max as the two men exited.

Gas filled the corridors as alarms sounded throughout the underground base.

"Guess we've been found out," Jefferson said.

Max pointed to the security cameras in the corners of the corridor. "Smile," Max said to Jefferson.

Two more guards rushed toward the brig, shock-sticks buzzing with controlled energy. Max, wearing one of the stolen helmets to protect him from the gas, leaped out from the mist and ripped their helmets off with ease.

They coughed and gasped for air before falling to the ground and passing out. Protected from the gas by their borrowed helmets, Max and Jefferson made their way to the control room.

Once inside, laser blasts danced at their feet. Max and Jefferson ran for cover. A guard stepped out in front of them. Jefferson hit him with a body block. The guard fell back into the console.

"Max, we've got to get out of here!" Jefferson yelled. A laser blast just missed his cheek.

"I'm on it," Max yelled back. "Get over here!"

Max was in the corner of the control room. He had found the hydraulic lift and its two guards. He punched one in the stomach and yanked off his helmet. He swung the helmet around, hard, and smacked the second guard in the head, shattering his helmet.

"Get ready, Mr. Smith," Max called out. "We're going out the way I came in."

Jefferson joined Max on the hydraulic platform. Max smacked a button on a nearby control panel. The trapdoor opened and the lift pushed father and son up toward the fresh air of Mount Corinth.

"This was too easy," Max observed. "Suddenly, all of the guards are gone. Like they're off doing something else. And their leader, that metal-face guy, he's gone, too."

Max shifted uncomfortably as they reached the out-doors and stood on top of Mount Corinth.

"There's something I haven't told you about that guy, yet, Dad."

Jefferson looked at Max curiously.

"He's the one," Max said nervously. "Mr. Security Breach from three months ago. The one I caught breaking into N-Tek."

"So, he's the man who created Max Steel by dumping those chemicals on you?"

Max could only nod in response.

12

Back at N-Tek, 'Berto was frantically trying to get his systems back on-line. His monitors were dark, Max was not responding to calls on the comlink, and the Bio-Link that charted Max's health was flat-lined.

Then Jefferson Smith, as seen through Max's eyes, popped up on the monitors. Max was back on-line.

"Max! You found him!" 'Berto said excitedly.

"Did you ever doubt me, bro?" Max leaped into the driver's side of his car as Jefferson opened the door and got in, shotgun. Max pressed a button on his Bio-Link, putting 'Berto on the speaker and on the car's video monitor.

'Berto examined his console. All systems were "go" again. "I've made a note of the area, sir," he said. "As soon as you're clear, we'll send in a cleanup team to take it down for good."

"And call back Mairot, Leeds, and the others, 'Berto," Jefferson commanded. "We're not finished yet."

"I know," 'Berto agreed. "All of this makes no sense to me . . . kidnapping you couldn't have been the goal. How would the missile attack play into that?"

"Assassination doesn't play, either," Max offered. "Or we'd both be history." Max turned the ignition, roaring his car to life.

"Someone knows that N-Tek is more than a sporting goods company, and that someone wanted N-Tek in chaos," Jefferson theorized. "And it didn't matter whether I was dead or just missing, as long as everyone was in a state of confusion and panic."

"Just as long as N-Tek's finest were lured out of town . . ." Max's brain was percolating as he and Jefferson buckled their seat belts.

"So who's the real target?" Jefferson asked. "Keita?"

"She's still under heavy guard," 'Berto said from the control room. "No way."

Max's car revved down Mount Corinth. The lights of Del

48

Oro Bay were visible and getting rapidly closer as Max accelerated.

"Then what else is going on down in Del Oro . . ." It finally clicked in Jefferson's head. Max got it, too. So did 'Berto.

"The virus!" they all yelled to one another at the same time.

Chapter

13

"Look, I've been waiting for forty-five minutes," Laura Chen said to the desk clerk at the University Bio-Research Center. "I know you don't usually handle cardiac patients . . ."

The desk clerk wasn't really listening. He was distracted by the array of security guards that were running behind him.

"But I've checked everywhere else," Laura pleaded. "Can you just tell me if there's a Jefferson Smith here?"

Outside the Bio-Research Center, two Dread attack helicopters hovered over the building. Rope ladders hung down to a large hole that had been blasted in the roof, revealing a chemical laboratory. The rooftop and the lab had been secured by Dread's minions . . . and Psycho.

"You don't know what you're taking," Dr. Yevshenko said to the smiling man with the metallic face. "The Cain Virus in that vessel has not been neutralized. Just a single drop of that solution can cause a plague —"

Psycho lifted up the Cain Virus containment vessel

from its stand behind the destroyed doors that used to keep it safe. The airtight golden container was small enough to be held in one hand.

"A plague that will destroy the human race!" Dr. Yevshenko yelled.

"Dread is counting on that, sister," Psycho snarled.

"I see the helicopters. That's not good."

Max and Jefferson approached the Bio-Research Center at top speed. Max had gunned Baby down Mount Corinth and sped toward Del Oro. That's when they had seen the Dread attack helicopters hovering over the building.

"Mairot is still twenty minutes away," Jefferson announced.

"Then we can't wait for the cavalry."

"Agreed. Let's cut off their escape before we go in," Jefferson instructed.

Max flipped a switch on Baby's dashboard. The trunk popped up and slid down into the car, out of the way. Two small rocket launchers rose from the trunk, rotated forward, aimed toward Del Oro.

"Targeting," Max said. The missiles were armed and ready. Simultaneously, he pressed two buttons on his dashboard. The rockets ignited and launched through the air.

They cut through the night sky, right toward the choppers. Impact! They struck the tail rotors of each one, exploding. A shower of sparks and flames cascaded below as the helicopter crews abandoned ship, leaping safely down to the roof.

Without their tail rotors, the flaming choppers spun out of control, down the side of the UBRC, and exploded in twin fireballs in the courtyard below. A burst of flame shot up almost five stories high.

Seconds later, Max and Jefferson pulled into the courtyard. Max looked up toward the roof and got out of the car.

"Could be a long wait for the elevator," he said.

"Ideas?"

Max reached back inside the car and flicked a switch.

The empty rocket-launchers rotated back into the trunk. Max reached in and pulled out two small jet packs. He hit a button on the side, and metallic wings, each about three feet long, extended out of the packs.

"Just a couple."

Chapter

14

"We've lost our choppers!"

In the lab, one of Psycho's henchmen called down through the hole in the roof. Psycho had lifted the containment vessel and with no effort at all, leaped through the hole and up onto the roof.

"Follow me! Move!" Psycho ordered.

Looking up at Psycho, one of the henchmen yelled, "You want hostages?" He pointed his shock-stick at Dr. Yevshenko and Dr. Ben-Rubin.

"Ha!" Psycho laughed as he held up the container of Cain Virus. "I have six billion hostages."

Now that he was on the roof, Psycho barked out orders. "Give me multiple lines! Now!"

The henchmen moved rapidly. They fired pitons into the roof and dropped cable reels off the sides of the UBRC building. They fastened the cables to their belts and dropped backward off the roof to rappel down to the ground.

But they hadn't counted on Max Steel! Max swooped above them, the wings on his jet pack guiding him with eaglelike precision. He scooped up the multiple cable lines

as he passed by. Screaming with shock and fear, the henchmen held onto their cables for dear life. Max rocketed straight up into the air, carrying them with him.

"Going *up*!"

Max was high above the UBRC when he changed direction and headed straight down toward the roof, like a dive-bomber on a strafing run.

"UBRC top floor: evil minions, crazy psychos, foiled plots . . ."

The roof was getting closer to Max and the henchmen in his grasp. Just before impact, Max cut the engines on his jet pack and dropped lightly onto the roof. The henchmen were not as lucky. They crashed onto the roof and lay in a pile, unconscious.

". . . and concrete."

Max didn't have time to enjoy the moment, however. Psycho ripped up a piece of the roof and hurled it at him. Max leaped to the side and the concrete chunk sailed past him. Before Max could recover from his jump, Psycho's foot pulverized his chest, knocking Max backward with enough force to crumple his jet pack. Max fell to the ground, knees first, but the rest of his body quickly followed.

Max struggled to get up, but the jolt had taken too much out of him. He needed time to recover, but Psycho wasn't going to give him any.

Intent on finishing the job, Psycho whipped out his shock-stick. Before he could jab Max, Jefferson jetted past, trying to grab the virus container. Psycho reacted quickly, dodging Jefferson's hands.

"Careful," Psycho threatened. "You wouldn't want me to drop this."

"If you drop it, we *all* die!" Jefferson yelled.

Psycho was joined by his remaining henchmen. "And yet, I don't seem to care," Psycho announced. "Must be why they call me Psycho! Let him have it, boys!"

The minions gave their wristbands a quarter turn. Their laser-gauntlets charged with energy and fired off multiple laser blasts from their closed fists.

Jefferson jumped through the air, dodging the blasts. He was good, but he was not as skilled a fighter as his son.

Max slowly regained his senses, but a large chromium claw clamped onto his chest and lifted him into the air. Max struggled but couldn't move. What he saw horrified him: The claw was actually part of Psycho's bionic arm.

"Wh — What *are* you?!" Max demanded.

"What's that line?" Psycho asked, even though he knew the answer. "Oh, yeah: 'Your worst nightmare'!"

The claw tightened. Max could feel his chest weakening. It wouldn't be long now before something inside snapped.

"Max! Snap out of it!" said 'Berto on the comlink. "You can take this guy!"

Max looked down on his Bio-Link. The button marked "Turbo" was within easy reach. Max's fingertips pressed it. Instantly, light radiated from his arms!

"If you say so, bro . . . GOING TURBO!"

The Max-Probes surged in Max's body, coursing through his veins and empowering him. He was stronger, more powerful, and it was time for payback.

Psycho was surprised by the energy display, even more surprised as the now-stronger Max forced the claw-arm open. Psycho's arm sparked and smoked. Steel tendons groaned like a broken elevator.

Max snapped the claw open. He dropped the few feet to

the roof and temporary safety. Psycho's claw-arm retracted and plopped to the roof as he backed away.

Max would have pursued him, but he had a more important obligation. The henchmen were still trying to shoot down Jefferson. Max knelt and slammed a turbo-charged fist into the damaged roof. Cracks appeared, wending their way under the henchmen. Suddenly, the roof opened up and the henchmen fell to the floor below, narrowly missing Dr. Yevshenko and Dr. Ben-Rubin, who scampered quickly out of the way.

"Hey, tough guy!" Psycho yelled from across the giant hole in the roof. "Aren't you forgetting something?" He held up the container of the virus.

"I don't forget anything," Max declared.

"C'mon," Psycho dared. "I've practically got one hand tied behind my back."

As he spoke, Jefferson jetted onto the roof, landing to one side of Psycho. He was surrounded.

"Two against me, huh? Guess I'll need two hands! So I won't need this anymore." Psycho swung the virus container over his head and released it. It sailed off the roof.

"NOOOOO!" Jefferson cried out, horrified. Knowing what would happen if that container hit the ground . . . Jefferson took to the air and dove after the virus. He was gaining on the falling container, but it was still out of reach.

Jefferson tried to speed up, stretching out every muscle in his body until it felt like his fingers were going to come off.

This is what it all came down to. No fancy gadgets, no secret weapons. The fate of the world depended on one man catching a falling container.

He got it! Quickly, Jefferson leveled off, inches from impact with the ground. But he turned too quickly, and the wings of his jet pack were sheared off by two streetlights. Helplessly, Jefferson crashed to the ground. He rolled, stuffing the container against his stomach to protect it.

When he finally came to a stop, he was only slightly bruised, his business suit torn. But the container . . . the container was safe. He held it with both hands.

Dad, you rule, Max thought to himself from up on the roof. Then he turned to face Psycho.

"Let's get down to business, Smiley. I've got a score to settle."

Only Psycho wasn't there. He was gone.

"I wasn't thrilled with today's little stunt," Max said to his father as he morphed back into Josh McGrath.

"Got results," Jefferson shrugged.

Josh and Jefferson had reached the smoldering lobby of the UBRC. Outside, firefighters were hosing down the burning helicopters. N-Tek's people were on the scene now and could handle the cleanup. The Cain Virus was back safely in their hands and had been moved to another lab for safekeeping.

"What happened to that Psycho guy?"

"I don't know, Josh," Jefferson said. "But I think we'll be seeing him again."

"I hope so," Josh replied. "I'd like that very much."

"Josh! Mr. Smith?!" It was Laura, running through the lobby toward them. She was stunned. "Are you all right? What happened here? Mr. Smith, I —"

"I'm fine, my dear," Jefferson explained calmly. "Just a minor case of angina, brought on by stress." He smiled toward Josh.

"And poor eating habits," Josh said. "Dad was just about to buy us a healthy breakfast."

"But the explosions! The crash . . ." Laura was freaking out as she pointed to the still-burning helicopters.

"Yeah, what was the deal with all of that?" Josh inquired.

"I have absolutely no idea," Jefferson said. "Maybe it'll be on the news tonight."

Laura looked at the surrounding disaster. Since she wasn't going to get any answers, she gave up. She hooked her arms through Josh's and Jefferson's and they exited the UBRC.

"Like father, like son," she joked. "Let's see about that breakfast."